九色鹿

THIS IS AN ARTHUR A. LEVINE BOOK

Published by Levine Querido

www.levinequerido.com · info@levinequerido.com

Levine Querido is distributed by Chronicle Books, LLC

Text and illustrations copyright © 2022 by Kailin Duan

Translation copyright © 2022 by Jeremy Tiang

Library of Congress Control Number: 2022931597

ISBN: 978-1-64614-178-4

Printed and bound in China

Published in September 2022

First Printing

Book design by Joy Chu

The text type was set in Adobe Garamond Pro

*Kailin Duan took inspiration from the famous Dunhuang frescoes,
so important to the history and culture of China. In order to create
a vivid color, and unique texture, she painted with a comprehensive
technique, involving acrylic, mineral color and Photoshop.*

九色鹿
nine color deer

Kailin Duan

TRANSLATED BY JEREMY TIANG

LQ

LEVINE QUERIDO

Montclair | Amsterdam | Hoboken

A very long time ago,

deep in the Kunlun Hills, there lived a mystical deer. Her antlers were white as snow, and her fur had nine different colors in it, so she was called the Nine Color Deer. She lived with her companion, a little bird, deep in the stillness of the forest, in a place no humans knew about.

One day, while roaming through the hills, the Nine Color Deer heard a cry for

help,

coming from a lake deep within the hills. Someone was drowning!

She ran towards the voice, through the wilderness,

over the hills, and across the winding river.

In the center of the lake, a young man struggled, about to be swallowed by the water. The Nine Color Deer sprang across the lake, leaping from wave to wave, until she had reached him.

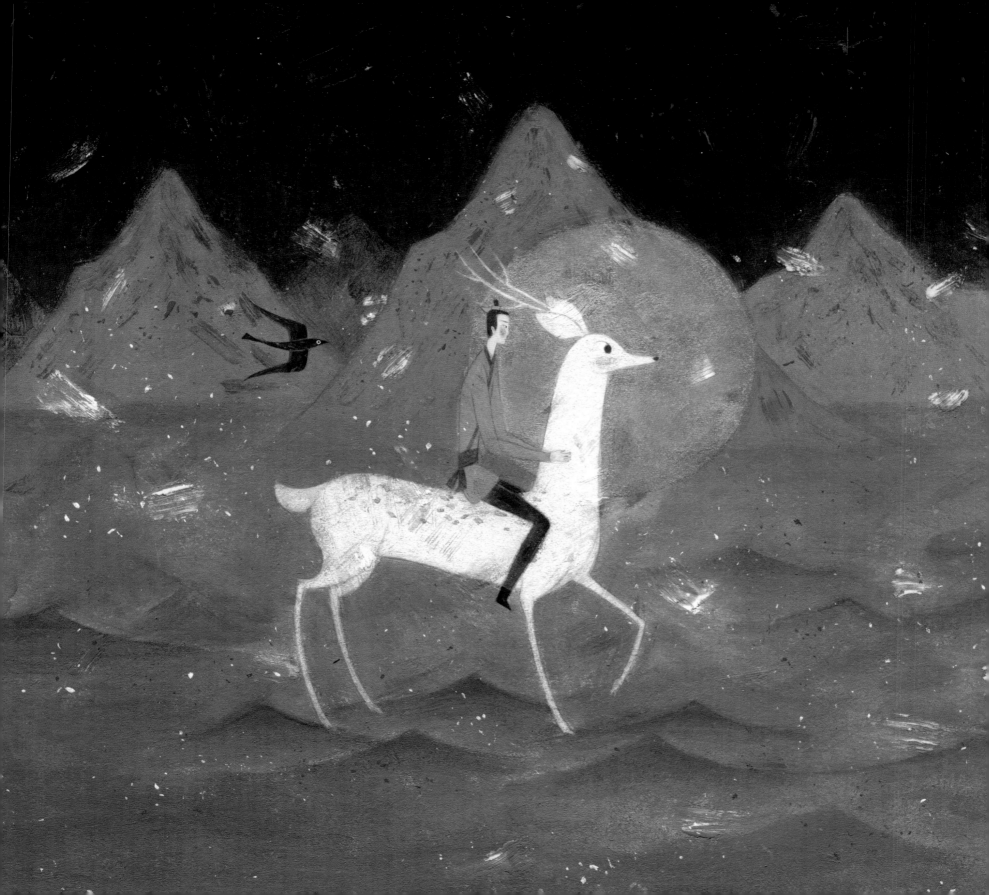

Together, they stepped lightly over the waves.

The young man cried, "How can I ever repay you for saving my life, oh noble deer?"

"All I ask," said the deer, "is that you tell no one of my whereabouts. Now hurry on home."

With that, the Nine Color Deer disappeared back into the forest.

The young man returned home

and didn't breathe a word
about what had happened to him—

that is, until news arrived from the imperial palace.

The king's beloved wife had been looking unhappy. Tenderly, he asked her, "My queen, what is it that troubles your heart?"

"A few days ago," the queen replied sadly, "I dreamed of a magical deer with nine colors in its fur.

Such a deer must surely have great powers—
a magnificent prize to help our kingdom prosper.
Can you find one?"

"Is that all?" said the king. "That shouldn't be too difficult. I'll summon my entire kingdom to help you find this deer."

Posters were plastered across the land, seeking the Nine Color Deer. When the young man saw the promised reward, he thought only of what the money would mean to his poor family, and forgot all about his promise to the deer.

The king and queen were delighted to hear what the young man had to say.
"The Nine Color Deer has magic powers," said the young man.
"You'll need to bring an army with you to capture it."

The king set forth with a large company of soldiers and horses, with the young man in front, leading the way. The sky darkened as they crossed the plains and went deep into the hills, startling the watchful little bird.

The little bird flew frantically back to the Nine Color Deer,
waking her from her nap—but it was too late.
There was no time to hide.

The king ordered his troops to surround
the Nine Color Deer and the little bird.

They lifted their bows,

took aim, and

fired.

The arrows flew towards the Nine Color Deer,
but before they could reach their target, a dazzling
white light blossomed around her, forcing the
king and his men to shield their eyes.

When they looked again, the arrows lay scattered and
broken on the ground.

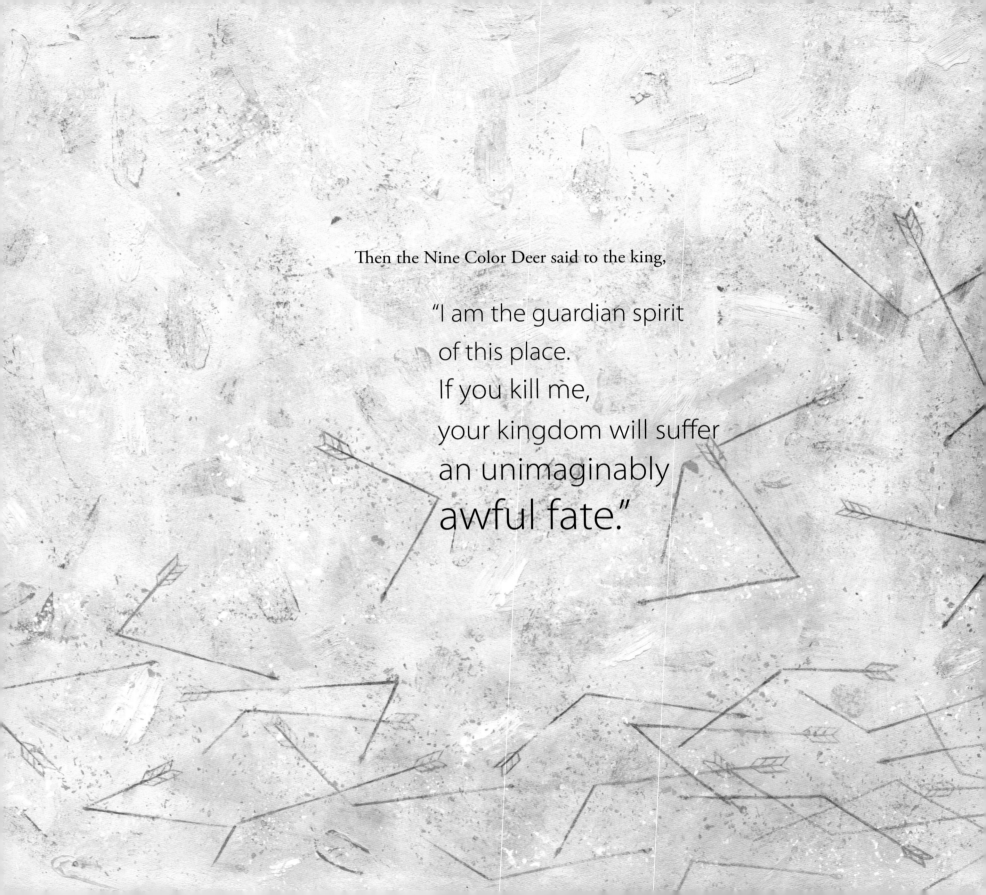

Then the Nine Color Deer said to the king,

"I am the guardian spirit
of this place.
If you kill me,
your kingdom will suffer
an unimaginably
awful fate."

The young man tried to hide behind the soldiers,
but the deer spotted him and said,

"Sir, I saved your life when you were drowning.

is this how you pay me back?"

Horribly ashamed, the young man knelt and begged for forgiveness. "I'm so sorry, kind deer," the young man cried, and he never broke a promise again.

The king rode home
and told his wife what
had happened.

"Thank goodness!"
said the queen.
"We almost made
a terrible mistake."
Together, they
ordered that no one
should ever harm
the Nine Color
Deer again.

Over time,
a mystical herd of deer
has begun to appear among
these hills. They all have nine colors
in their fur. As always, the little black bird
watches over them, and the country
continues to flourish to this day.

TRANSLATOR'S NOTE

Rendering this story into English was only one of many types of translation that bring you this edition of nine color deer, a story with a long history. Even as I worked from Kailin Duan's vivid text, I was aware that she had "translated" the illustrative style of this tale from one of the Mogao Cave paintings in Dunhuang, China. This particular wall painting, dating to over a thousand years ago, was in turn inspired by a Buddhist Jataka tale from India. All in all, from the very first iteration of the story to this version, roughly two thousand years have passed. The Nine Color Deer is certainly very long-lived, if not immortal, to have lasted all that time. The queen in the story might have been right about the deer's great powers.

The Chinese scholar Yu Qiuyu says that "to see the Mogao Caves is to witness not a specimen that's been dead a thousand years, but a life that has flourished for a millennium." Although some of the wall paintings in these grottoes are over 1,500 years old, others only appeared after that, layer by layer, and these images "were constantly being added to, restored and expanded, growing into a living entity that breathes, metabolizes, ages and spawns new generations."

From this wealth of myth and legend, Kailin Duan has chosen one tale to bring to new readers. Her evocative illustrations are clearly influenced by the characteristic style of the original cave painting, while also being infused with a spirit all of their own. While the Mogao Caves might now be preserved as relics, it seems we are still capable of building upon the images within them. I hope you will enjoy the story of the Nine Color Deer—long may her spirit live on.

九色鹿